Praise for *The Personal History, Adventures, Experiences & Observations of Peter Leroy:*

"Precisely literate." — *The Boston Globe*

"Introduces America to a major new humorist." — *Newsday*

"The sex is bracing and the boating can't be beat." — *Philadelphia Inquirer*

"A little world, full of absurdity and clamshells, but warm and loving, too." — *The Village Voice*

"These books carry ... a profound sense of literary lineage." — *Women's Wear Daily*

"Lake Woebegone as conceived by a modern Marcel Proust." — *The Christian Science Monitor*

"Funny, lighthearted, and sexy." — *St. Petersburg Times*

"Bright, light, satirical, fun." — *The Boston Review*

"Reaffirms the vitality of our own authors in a world of throw-away literature." — *The Santa Cruz Sentinel*

"A comic masterpiece." — *The Boston Phoenix*

"Satirizes everything from 19th-century novels to fast food." — *The New York Times*

The
PERSONAL HISTORY,
ADVENTURES, EXPERIENCES
&
OBSERVATIONS
of

PETER LEROY
A SERIES OF NOVELS BY ERIC KRAFT

1985
Apple-wood Books
Cambridge/Watertown

ISBN: 0-918222-62-1

*The Personal History, Adventures, Experiences &
Observations of Peter Leroy* is a work of fiction. The
people in it do not exist, nor have they ever existed.
Any resemblance to persons living or dead is uninten-
tional and coincidental.

10 9 8 7 6 5 4 3 2 1

For Mad

*Though we do not wholly believe it yet, the interior
life is a real life, and the intangible dreams of
people have a tangible effect on the world.*

James Baldwin

*. . . are there perhaps other worlds more real than
the waking world? . . . Often we have before us, in
those first minutes in which we allow ourself to slip
into the waking state, a truth composed of different
realities among which we imagine that we can
choose, as among a pack of cards.*

Marcel Proust
"Life with Albertine"
The Captive
(Translated by C. K. Scott Moncrieff)

*Eric Kraft . . . looks exactly like my mind's-eye
picture of Peter Leroy: wiry build, wacky smile,
bright eyes.*

Susan Orlean
"Getting Serial"
The Boston Phoenix

Preface

MY RELATIONSHIP with Larry Peters is a complex one. In the simplest terms, I owe my livelihood to him, but, far more than that, I owe to the series of adventure novels in which Larry has appeared for some thirty years—and to their pseudonymous authors—the discovery of an avenue to a feeling of artistic freedom without which I think that I would never have managed to write any of my personal history, adventures, experiences, and observations.

In the pages that follow, I have tried to narrate the origin of that relationship and explain its complexity. I fear that in the process I may have slighted the authors of the original Larry Peters books. That was never my intention. Because I know far too well how much effort goes into the writing of even the thinnest books, I would never intentionally belittle it.

Peter Leroy
Small's Island
December 10, 1984

1

I WAS BARELY adolescent when I first encountered Larry Peters, the eponymous hero of a series of books called, collectively, The Adventures of Larry Peters. My maternal grandmother, Gumma, gave me the first book in the series, *The Shapely Brunette*, as a present and a consolation, when I was sick, confined to bed, on my birthday. I had one of the childhood diseases, but I can't recall now which one it was: measles, mumps, chicken pox, or the twenty-four-hour virus. These illnesses were not so bad, I thought. The discomfort that they brought was part of growing up, each made one a little more grown up, and the knowledge that one gained from them ranked in the upper third or so of things that were, at that age and time, important to know: if one did not know at first hand what the pain of mumps was like, one was not an initiate into a certain shadowy nook of childhood experience that those outside it wanted to enter. That it might be nice not to have to be intitiated into that particular corner of childhood experience at all did not occur to me then. It would have been more painful, at the time, to be excluded from it, and so I welcomed the mumps, the experience of mumps, the knowledge of mumps.

There was even an aspect of illness that I enjoyed. I liked having to stay in bed for hours on end, left to myself, left to amuse myself. At that time, before my mother became an independent businesswoman, she was at home for most of the day, cleaning the house and cooking. She would come into my room from time to time to see if I needed anything, but for most of the day she was busy with her own occupations, and so I had time to myself, time to think, time to let my mind wander, time just to enjoy being alone; and when my mother left the house, as she did for at least part of each day, to go shopping or do other chores or to visit a friend, I had the house to myself. I had formed the habit, at an early age, of reading in bed, so it was a treat to have all day to do it, in my own bed, in my own room, and, best of all, in a silent and empty house. In the morning, my mother would give me breakfast in bed: toast and cocoa, hot cereal with evaporated milk, or graham crackers broken into milk. I would listen to the radio while I ate, usually to a program called "Bob Balducci's Breakfast Bunch," which was supposed to originate from a restaurant, Bob Balducci's, famous for its pancakes and waffles. The program was a variety show, with singers and comedians, and with guests who spoke on subjects that they knew at least something about; all of that was interesting enough, but my favorite part came late in the program, when Bob Balducci and his sidekick, Baldy the Talking Dummy, had the people in the audience–a group that seemed, from his interviews with representatives of it, to consist entirely of grandmothers–stand beside their chairs and perform calisthenics. My mental image of this performance was so vivid and so hilarious that on some mornings it made me laugh until I cried, and I would have to set my tray on my bedside table as soon as Baldy the Dummy announced in his everlastingly ebullient style, "Now it's time to get up off those (pause) chairs!" I knew that if I didn't set my tray aside, I was sure to spill my breakfast when I began laughing. When I had finished eating, I would sit up, with several pillows propped behind me, and read.

At noon, I'd have clam chowder, tomato soup, or chicken noodle soup with saltine crackers that I would either break into pieces and scatter over the top of the soup or eat in single bites that I alternated with spoonfuls of soup, and I would listen to the radio while I ate, listening at this time of the day to soap operas, my favorite of which was "Mary Backstage, Noble Wife." After lunch, I would read some more, play with my plaster Babbingtonians, listen to the radio, and doze.

I should explain about those plaster Babbingtonians. At Jack's Twenty-Four Hour Jokes, on the southwest corner of Bolotomy and Main, one could buy, and most of us between the ages of nine and twelve did buy, modeling kits called "Virtues 'n' Vices," which contained red rubber molds and plaster of Paris, with which one could cast figures that represented the Cardinal Virtues and the Seven Deadly Sins. I had quite a collection of these figures, most of them imperfect, with holes where bubbles had formed when I filled the mold, or with an arm glued ineptly back on after it had broken in the unmolding. From the first, I had noticed resemblances between the figures and various people around town. In fact, I found that by making a few simple modifications, working with one of my mother's emery boards, a Popsicle stick, and some fresh plaster, I could construct, out of Wisdom, Courage, Temperance, Justice, Faith, Hope, Charity, Pride, Covetousness, Lust, Anger, Gluttony, Envy, and Sloth, convincing likenesses of nearly everyone I knew or observed. A little work with some tempera paint made the likenesses even more convincing. I enjoyed manipulating these replica Babbingtonians, pairing them, grouping them, imagining conversations and arguments among them. (Years later, I learned that Jack sold other molds as well, but only to older boys and girls, molds from which one could cast figures of men and women that could be combined in interesting sexual positions. When I learned this, two thoughts came immediately to my mind: first, that it must have taken much greater skill than I possessed to unmold these figures and, second, that modifying them to make them resemble Babbingtonians must have been more complicated than modifying the "Virtues 'n' Vices" had been.)

At night, during times when I was ill, I would put on my plaid flannel bathrobe and join my mother and father for dinner, and then I would return to bed to read some more, draw pictures, write notes to the friends I wasn't able to visit or see in school, put my plaster Babbingtonians away, listen to the radio some more—most often to mystery programs—and doze. There are certainly worse ways to spend one's days.

2

I WAS ENCHANTED by that first Larry Peters adventure, *The Shapely Brunette*, from the moment that I opened the book. On the front end-paper was a map of the area where Larry lived, a seacoast town called Murky Bay. The town of Murky Bay was situated on the

shore of the bay called Murky Bay, and in Murky
Bay were hundreds of islands, among them one
called Kittiwake Island, where the Peters family
lived. On the back end-paper was a map of the
island itself and the floor plans of the Peters
house and the workshops where Mr. Peters and
the employees of Peters's Knickknacks worked in
secrecy to develop the gewgaws, trinkets, baubles,
bric-a-brac, curios, gimcrackery, and brum-
magems that were the Peterses' bread and butter.
I spent quite some time with the maps and floor
plans before I began reading the book, and I
returned to them often while I was reading it.
There was something about those maps and floor
plans that invited the mind to wander, to mean-
der among the islets as one might in a rowboat, to
prowl around the house looking for hidden
nooks, to imagine the conversations one might
have with a companion while meandering among
the islets or while hiding in a nook. The maps and
floor plans were detailed enough to seem to
depict real places, and yet they were vague
enough not to impose on me the limitations of
reality, and, since I knew that they did not depict
real places, they permitted—even invited—the
fabrication of imaginary details, since those
details had only to fit the empty spaces provided
for them and be in keeping with the details that
were already there; they did not have to be
verifiable. Often, later, while I was rereading, the

stories themselves seemed too specific; at such times, I found myself returning to the end-papers, and I began making up new stories for myself. Surely, I thought, these schematics were deliberately designed to encourage this kind of dreaming, and surely the stories were intended only to give one an excuse for sitting still for long hours, imagining new goings-on on Kittiwake Island, imagining the voices across the Peters dinner table, the debates that must have taken place in the knickknack workrooms, and so on.

The frontispiece to that first book showed two boys, Larry Peters and his friend Rocky King, square-jawed American boys, standing side by side in a fierce wind, the collars of their wind-breakers or flight jackets up, their hair blowing in a style that became popular in men's clothing advertisements much later in my life. Rocky was holding a large pair of binoculars to his eyes and peering into the darkness. In that darkness, one could see a lighted window, and in that lighted window, one could make out, if one studied the illustration closely and carefully enough, a shapely woman, presumably the brunette of the title. Larry was reaching for the binoculars, and under the illustration was a line from the book:

"Come on, Rocky," Larry pleaded. "It's my turn."

I read *The Shapely Brunette* twice that day, and a third time the next day. Then I read every other Larry Peters book that had been published. From then on, I waited impatiently for new books to come out. I was hooked on Larry Peters, and I wanted my friends to share my enthusiasm. I wanted them to read the books, to read them as thoroughly as I had read them, to absorb them as I had, so that we could use them in our friendship, use them as a constant, a given, in our conversations together, add them to the context of our conversations for the same reasons that one adds manure to garden soil: so that the plants will flourish, grow thick and intertwined, flower profusely and brilliantly. But most of my friends didn't share my enthusiasm for Larry Peters, his adventures, Kittiwake Island, or the habit of mingling reading with dreaming. They didn't notice everything that I noticed. Most didn't even recognize, in the frontispiece to *The Shapely Brunette*, the image of the shapely brunette in the lighted window.

"Wishful thinking," said Raskolnikov. "That's just a way of drawing. The artist uses a few quick strokes of the pen to suggest that the shade is down without inking in the whole shade. We had that in art class already. It's just an artist's trick; it's not really meant to represent anything. You only see a woman there because you want to." He jabbed me in the ribs.

3

I RETURNED to the Larry Peters books again and again because the Peters family, Kittiwake Island, Murky Bay, and the ambience of potential adventure were so fecund a ground for the imagination. The adventures themselves became, for me, only the trellises on which each book grew. The stories were there to hold the books together, prop them up, but that function, although useful, perhaps even necessary, wasn't interesting; it could have been fulfilled by any story, as far as I was concerned, any story at all. The vines that grew on these trellises were much, much more interesting, and part of the interest that I took in them came from the fact that I was partly responsible for making them grow. Certainly the author, Roger Drake, was responsible for the stock, the planting, fertilizing the ground, but it was I who sent tendrils off at unpredictable spots, who sent the vines wandering in several directions, who made them blossom.

I didn't dislike the adventures, of course, but their attraction faded quickly. They were exciting to read the first time, considerably less exciting the second time, and not particularly exciting at all after that. Exactly the reverse was true of what each book told me about Larry, his home and family, his surroundings, and his friend Rocky King, matters that on first reading seemed to be only part of the background for the adventures, a sketchy background at that, but became more and more interesting as I read and reread.

The reader was not given much direct information about the personal, the private side of Larry's life. Now and then, a tantalizing piece of information would pop up in the course of an adventure, but more often there were simply gaps in the narrative that invited one to fill them. For example, in the adventure called *Bamboozled!* Larry and Rocky and Mr. Peters chase a mysterious prowler across the island, dashing through a labyrinth of bamboo that Larry has planted to baffle such prowlers. During a long and complicated night, the three become separated in the maze and are lost for several hours while the prowler makes his way to the knickknack works, rifles the file cabinet containing the plans for next year's line of gewgaws, and makes off with the Peterses' speedboat. When, finally, the boys and Mr. Peters are reunited and realize what has happened, Mr. Peters pounds them on the back, assures them that they did their best, tells them that he's counting on them to track the prowler down while he and the designers come up with a new line of gewgaws, and then says, "Boys, it will be dawn in another hour or so, and we've got quite a day ahead of us. What do you say we get an hour's sleep, have a swim and a shower, and put away one of your mother's famous hearty breakfasts?" That is the end of the chapter. The next chapter opens with Larry and Rocky crouched outside a boathouse, peering through a window at a gang of thugs in the employ of a rival knickknack company. But for me, a great deal happened between the chapters. I had, ever since Mr. Beaker first taught me to read, been in the habit of filling whatever gaps appeared in whatever I was reading. The Adventures of Larry Peters seemed to have been written just for someone who had developed this habit, just for me. The books were full of gaps, some small, some big enough to wander in for days at a time. I filled this particular one with a conversation in Larry's bedroom, a swim, a glimpse of Larry's sister Lucinda in the shower, a breakfast of blueberry pancakes and sausage, the boys' goodbyes, their running out of gas on the way across Murky Bay, the Coast Guard's towing them to the town dock, a friend who lent them a jalopy (an amusing fellow who was always trying to get Larry's sister to go to the movies with him), a dented fender, a flat tire, a Pullman diner, a redheaded waitress with freckles and teary eyes, and much, much more.

4

THE PETERS FAMILY seemed, to me, quite rich, rich in all the ways that I would have considered a family rich at that time. They owned a whole island, after all. They had a maid, about whom I will have more to say later. They owned three boats: a working boat, a barge really, that they used for carrying freight from the mainland, and, in *The Missing Garage*, used to transport an entire Esso gas station; a sailboat, a lean blue sloop, that Larry was permitted to sail by himself and on which Larry's sister enjoyed sunning herself; and a speedboat, a mahogany Chris Craft speedboat with a twelve-cylinder engine. On the mainland, they owned a small piece of waterfront property in the town of Murky Bay, where they had a dock, a boathouse for the speedboat, and a garage in which they kept a Jaguar Saloon and a war-surplus Jeep.

Everything that the Peterses did was of an order different from anything my family or the families of any of my friends did. My father might spend most of a Saturday changing the oil and filter in our aging Commander, trying to devise a scheme to make my mother's washing machine stop walking across the cellar floor, or painting the garage, but Mr. Peters was likely to spend a Saturday tied up in the hold of a sinking ship, rappeling down a rock face in pursuit of some bric-a-brac smugglers, or conducting delicate negotiations for the purchase of some fine amber in Lübeck.

And the meals! Every time the Peters family sat down to a meal, it seemed to be the kind of meal that I associated with festivals and celebrations and funerals. If they were having breakfast, they drifted into the dining room one by one, and each filled a plate from a sideboard laden with oatmeal, pancakes, bacon, sausages (sometimes of two kinds), coffee, cocoa, milk, juices, sticky buns, crumb cake, crullers, bran muffins, bagels, kaiser rolls, English muffins, toasted rye bread, toasted raisin bread, jelly doughnuts, white mountain rolls, corn muffins, salt sticks, bialys, and fruit. Marie, the maid, would fix eggs any way anyone wanted them. At home, my father usually started the day with white toast, coffee, and a couple of cigarettes. My mother rarely had more than coffee. I usually had a bowl of graham crackers soaked in milk, sometimes a cup of cocoa and toast.

Dinner at the Peterses' was always a big deal: baked ham, turkey, a roast beef, bowls of potatoes and vegetables, everyone talking away and eating like mad. Of course, they had to eat a lot when they could, because most of the meals at the Peters house were never finished. No sooner would they get their plates heaped with food and eat a few healthy bites than someone would begin shooting at the house from a low-flying plane, an explosion on the mainland would rattle the windows, or Marie would announce the arrival of a mysterious stranger. Dinners were sometimes interrupted in my family, too, but the interruptions seemed to me, at the time, less likely to lead to anything interesting: the heating pipes would begin making metallic knocking sounds, but upon investigation we would find no dark-eyed waif tied up in the cellar, banging on the pipes to rouse some help, only air in the radiators; we'd be startled by a knock at the back door, but it was never a mysterious stranger, only the Mr. Doughboy delivery man, running late on his route; a flash of light would fill the room, and a moment later an explosive crash would rattle the windows, but it would only be a summer thunderstorm, and in those days a summer storm was not as exciting as an exploding gimcrack factory.

5

LARRY WAS NEVER BORED. That is, he was never bored within the books. I knew from experience that everyone my age was bored for a significant amount of time every day. It may have been the absence of boredom that made me truly understand how much of Larry's life was missing from The Adventures of Larry Peters, that made me begin to understand how distorted was the picture of Larry's life that we, the readers, Larry's admirers, were allowed to see. It seemed safe to assume that the Peters family ate dinner every evening, or nearly every evening. Logic told me that not all of these dinners could be interrupted by events that were part of one adventure or another. There had to be dinners when no one had much to say, when Larry poked at his peas with his fork, watched a skin form on his gravy, and didn't hear his father asking him what he was daydreaming or moping about.

Not only was Larry never bored within the books, but he was always busy. He was always working on one project or another, and taking the trash out was never one of them. Larry seemed very clever to me, as he must have to all readers, as he was intended to seem, and yet for all his cleverness, for all the things he knew, for all his work on one arcane project or another, he managed to be an all-round guy. He could make a good showing in a fight, even against hired thugs, run like a deer when the situation required it, climb cliffs or warehouse walls, tap phone lines, swim, fish, play chess. In fact, I had the idea, an idea encouraged by most of the things that occurred in the books, that there was probably nothing that a boy my age might want to do that Larry couldn't do. If Larry never sang or danced or played the clarinet or baked a soufflé or cast sculpture in bronze or flew an airplane, it wasn't because he couldn't, it was simply because he didn't feel like it or because the occasion for doing so hadn't yet arisen in one of his adventures. In fact, I now recall that he did bake a soufflé and fly an airplane in *The Aerobatic Sous-Chef.*

6

LARRY'S FRIEND, buddy, *copain*, comrade, Rocky King, was the perfect pal for someone like Larry—or for someone like me.

He was big and strong, older, a young man more than a boy; he had a past about which we knew little, other than the fact that he had lost his parents at an early age and had had to shift for himself, a necessity that had toughened him. When he first appeared on the scene, in that very first book, *The Shapely Brunette*, it was to come to Larry's aid, much as Arthur comes to the aid of Guyon in *The Faerie Queene* (Book II, Canto VIII).

Larry walked quickly along the wet streets, his footsteps echoing against the squalid houses on either side. Now and then he thought that he caught sight of a face in one of the windows, spotted a puff of smoke exhaled behind a shutter, or heard a murmured remark as he passed. Then, from an archway to his right, came a small voice, a small voice straining to sound strong.

"Hey, what's your hurry?" asked the voice.

Larry snapped his head around and saw, in the shadowy archway, the face of girl no older than he. Her hair was straight, the color of a fawn's ears, and it needed combing. Her eyes were bright, even in the darkness, but they looked out from deep recesses darkened with kohl. She looked terribly tired, despite her smile, despite the way she tilted her head so that her pointed chin showed to best advantage. She reached out toward him.

"It's cold," she said. "Wet, too. Why don't you come inside?"

"I'd like to," said Larry, "but—." He stopped himself. He had to be careful. He had almost let slip the fact that he was searching for a gang of Turkish gewgaw smugglers. He had to remember that he couldn't afford to trust anyone.

"It's warm inside," she said. "We can have fun together." She spread the shawl that she had wrapped around her, opening it as an angel might spread her wings. In the shadows, Larry could just make out the pale whiteness of her skin. As if in a dream, he moved toward her.

"Hold it, sailor," said a strong voice behind Larry. A hand as strong as the voice gripped his shoulder and held him back; something in that grip, something strangely fraternal, told Larry that the hand that held him back was the hand of a friend, an ally. "Get lost, sister," said the unknown friend to the girl in the shadows. The girl closed the shawl around her, twisted her mouth into a sneer and then spat on the paving stones at Larry's feet, turned and disappeared through a dark doorway. From the same doorway, a stocky, swarthy, unshaven man emerged; clearly this man was no friend. In the stocky man's hand was a cleaver. Larry heard a metallic click behind his ear, and the strong arm of his unknown protector pushed him to one side, against the stone building. From an open window somewhere above him Larry heard the sharp, staccato notes of a zither. Larry's mysterious ally was silhouetted against the light from a streetlamp, and Larry could see that in one strong hand he held a revolver.

"Get lost, Bud," snarled the strong but oddly friendly voice of the young man who had come to Larry's aid. Larry saw the swarthy man bare his teeth, but he retreated into the shadows, and Larry heard a door close. "Come on, kid," said the friendly stranger. "Let's get out of here."

Later, when they sat in the relative safety of a rough waterfront café, warming themselves over steaming mugs of cocoa, Larry struggled to find the words to thank the young man who had come to his aid.

"I don't know how to thank you." he began.

"Forget it, kid," said the smiling young man.

"I don't even know your name," said Larry.

"Call me Rocky," said the young man, smiling broadly and extending his large and callused right hand across the table.

"Call me Larry," said Larry, smiling as broadly as he could, reaching across the table to shake Rocky's hand and knocking the young man's cocoa into his lap.

Certainly Rocky impressed Larry and the reader with his strength, his predisposition to act, to do something about whatever situation arose, even if he did not often take the time to consider whether what he was doing was in every respect, in all its ramifications, right. More surprising, however, and for me at least more welcome, was the fact that Rocky was continually impressed by qualities of Larry's that the reader may not have thought impressive, qualities that many readers— this one, certainly—may have possessed themselves but counted as nearly worthless since their playmates and schoolmates considered them of little value, may even have counted them as shortcomings before they saw that Rocky admired them in Larry. Among these was Larry's indecisiveness, which Rocky took as laudable evidence not merely of Larry's ability to see all sides of a question and all the consequences of an action, but also of his feeling that he had an intellectual obligation to do so.

"We'll go in through the French doors," said Rocky, "get the will out of the safe, make our getaway through the topiary garden, and then call your father from the pay phone back at that godforsaken gas station and beanery we passed out there in the middle of nowhere."

"I'm not sure that's the best plan, Rocky," said Larry, his eyelids lowered in an attitude of thought. "What if the will isn't in the safe? Suppose there are *two* safes in the house? We know that these people are quite rich, and if *I* were quite rich and had a big house like this, I'd have two safes: one for jewels and one for cash and valuable papers. Now the obvious thing to do would be to put the one for jewels in a bedroom, or in a dressing room, and put the one for valuable papers in the library. But if I've learned one thing about Kurt Politzer, it's that he's too smart to do the obvious thing. The safe in the library here probably doesn't have any valuable papers in it at all. In fact, I wouldn't be surprised if the papers were in the safe in the dressing room." Suddenly Larry's face lit up, and he began shaking his head in an attitude of grudging admiration for their adversary. "No," he said. "No. There are *three* safes. *Of course.* This safe has nothing valuable in it at all. There *is* a third safe, and it's probably tucked away somewhere where no one would expect a safe to be. In the kitchen, maybe. Or in the nursery. Or in a bathroom. I'll bet that's it; the safe we want is in a bathroom. I'll bet I even know *which* bathroom it is: it's the guest bathroom, the powder room, and I'll bet it's on this floor. Perfect, perfect. All the most valuable papers are in a place that most people, certainly most thieves, would think wasn't safe at all: *behind the mirror in the powder room.* Oh, there are probably some papers in the safe here in the library, some non-negotiable stock certificates, passports, things like that, so that a thief who broke into this safe wouldn't look for another one, would just figure that the jewels and other valuables were in a safe-deposit box. *A safe-deposit box!*" Larry snapped his fingers, and a group of dogs began barking. "Of course, Rocky!" he shouted. Suddenly, floodlights lit the grounds of the Politzer mansion. "The will isn't in the house at all!" said Larry. "It's in a safe-deposit box somewhere!"

Rocky also admired Larry's academic talents. He never ceased to be amazed at how quick and clever Larry was, not that Rocky was less quick or less clever, but Rocky's talents and knowledge were more restricted to practical areas: he could overhaul the engine in the Jeep with only a nail file and a can opener as tools, and he could find the best place to get a cheap and decent meal in most of the world's ports; yet Rocky, although he was older than Larry, seemed to know a lot less about the things one might be expected to learn in school than Larry did. This shortcoming of Rocky's wasn't explained, but I decided that it must have to do with that past of Rocky's about which we knew so little. I supposed that in his past there had been a reform school, from which Rocky had run away before he'd had a chance to pick up much long division or world history. Rocky's ignorance of what one learned in school gave Larry the opportunity, frequently, to explain something to Rocky that would impress the heck out of him and would make the reader, who was likely already to know what Larry explained, feel all the more like Larry and to think of himself as in some ways a leader or even a protector of big, friendly, uneducated lugs like Rocky.

7

LARRY'S FATHER was everything a boy might hope for, a real paterfamilias, who considered himself in control, who entertained few doubts about himself, who assumed that he was the true head of the Peters ménage. But beyond that, his work made him unusual as fathers go: he was an artist of sorts. His artistic impulses had two manifestations. One was the knickknack business, of course, and that could be considered one of the practical or applied arts; the other, the purer manifestation, was his making life interesting for himself and for his family.

Mr. Peters was able to do many things, and he got many things done. He was well known and admired for many of the things that he did. Others of the things that he attempted did not have the results that he or anyone else involved in the endeavor might have hoped for, but they always resulted in a richer, more various, more interesting life for the Peterses. Within the Peters family, not an eyebrow would be raised if Mr. Peters announced, over dinner one evening, that in the morning everyone would begin building a raft so that the family could chart the course of the Gulf Stream during their vacation, or that he had a plan for a sling that could be hung inside a suburban garage, onto which the suburban motorist could drive his car, and which, thanks to an ingenious system of gears driven by the car's rear wheels, would rock the motorist's colicky infant offspring gently to sleep, or that he intended to import minks to the island, where, since there were no predators, they could be allowed to run free and would breed quickly, making the Peterses wealthy beyond imagining.

And yet, as unpredictable and impracticable as Mr. Peters's schemes may sometimes have been, he had a steady, responsible side too. The business savvy he displayed as the head of a world-renowned knickknack design firm was a world apart from the world of late nights, cheap wine, and strong cigarettes that is so firmly established in the popular notion of bric-a-brac designers. The knickknack business, as portrayed in the Larry Peters books, was a tense, competitive, cutthroat business, much more exciting than most businesses that my father or the fathers of my friends were in or were ever likely to get themselves into. Mr. Peters had moved his family to Kittiwake Island because he needed secrecy, he needed a place where he could develop his designs without his competitors' learning about them before they were released. However, his competitors were a ruthless, unprincipled bunch who would stop at nothing to steal his designs or sabotage his plans: that's how the adventures arose.

Mr. Peters was inventive, a leader, a loving father, and more; he was something that .most fathers of my acquaintance were not: a dignified man. One could see, too, that he bore as if he were a block of granite the cares that can fall on any family, taking the full weight, so that life should rest lightly on the shoulders of the others. The reader saw this quality at once, when he first met Mr. Peters in his study in *The Shapely Brunette*.

Larry knew that he would find his father in the tiny attic study to which Edgar Peters retired when he needed to think and work undisturbed. Larry stopped outside the door and knocked; everyone on Kittiwake Island knew that Edgar Peters was not to be burst in upon when he was concentrating in his attic retreat.

"Just a minute," said the voice of Marie, the maid. Larry waited impatiently, snapping the nails of the thumb and middle finger of each hand together in his eager agitation. From behind the door came muffled conversation, the sound of something scraping along the floor. At last the door opened, and Marie, flushed, breathing heavily, the rounded tops of her ample breasts heaving above the neckline of her little black chintz maid's dress, stepped out of Edgar Peters's attic asylum. "Oh, it's you Larry," she said. "Your father is deep in thought. I was just straightening up around him and—"

She turned suddenly and looked back into the little hideaway. She scampered back inside and emerged with her feather duster.

"—dusting," she finished, flourishing the feather duster. She giggled and started down the stairs.

Larry stepped inside his father's narrow lair. Gewgaws were everywhere—along the radiator, on shelves, and tossed indiscriminately on the floor. The walls were lined with cartons of letters from correspondents around the world, all on the subject of knickknacks, the bread and butter of the Peters clan. Just inside the door were displayed documents declaring that Edgar Lawrence Peters was a member of the National Institute of Bric-a-brac Designers, an honorary member of the *Institut des Fabricateurs des Bibelots,* and an honorary fellow of the Royal Academy of Curio Makers. He had won awards from the Gewgaw Fanciers and the Chatchke Mavens, among others. On the knickknack ladder, Edgar Peters was tops.

Crammed into one corner, positioned to take advantage of the light from the only window, was a rickety table that served Mr. Peters as a desk. To the casual eye, the desk, heaped with market research reports, rough sketches, and prototypes of next year's line of gimcrackery from the Peters group, suggested a disorganized and haphazard thinker, but Larry knew that his father possessed a fine analytical mind, and that the disarray was deliberate, calculated to disarm visitors.

Dressed in one of the rumpled tweed suits that he wore in the belief that they gave him a learned air, Edgar Peters was mussing his thick sandy hair with one hand and tracing the lines of an intricate sketch with the other.

Larry wanted his father's attention, but he was reluctant to disturb his concentration, so he stood across the table from him, fidgeting.

Father and son shared the most pronounced Peters family features: a wiry build, a wacky smile, and bright eyes. Larry shared his father's affectations too: rumpling his hair now and then as if absent-mindedly, and dressing in professorial tweeds, usually a herringbone suit, though Larry's tweeds were often considerably spotted with oil paints, which Larry considered a bohemian touch. Mr. Peters thought that the boy lacked polish.

Edgar Peters looked up from his work at last. He peered at Larry over the top of his glasses, as parents of adolescents (parents who wear glasses) will sometimes do. "Oh, Larry," he said. "What's up, son?"

Larry chuckled. "You certainly were deep in concentration, Dad," he said. "You didn't even know that I was here. I'll bet you never even noticed that Marie was in here, trying to straighten up and do some dusting."

Mr. Peters reddened, and Larry wished that he

hadn't said anything, for it was apparent to him that his father was embarrassed by his being, as Larry's mother so often said, "in another world" when he was concentrating on a gimcrack design.

"Yes—well—I—I—" Mr. Peters's voice trailed off, and he rumpled his hair. "Did you want something, Larry?" he asked.

"Can you spare a minute to take a look at my latest project, Dad?" asked Larry.

Edgar Peters removed his glasses and slipped them into his jacket pocket. He rubbed the spatulate indentations on either side of his nose. "I could use a break," he said with a weary sigh. "These damned sketches are giving me a headache." With a sweep of his hand he indicated the plans that covered his desk.

"Aren't they any good?" asked Larry.

"On the contrary," said Mr. Peters. "They're more than good. They're brilliant, innovative, ambitious." He let out another weary sigh. "That's the problem." He indicated the clutter on his desk. "These are the sketches for next year's line. Your Uncle Hector thinks we can make bivalves the next knickknack rage, bigger than the little rococo courtiers we've done so well with, bigger than the black ceramic panthers, bigger even than the flamingos. Perhaps he's right, but frankly it's an enormous risk. Who can really be sure what piece of bric-a-brac people will want next? And these are supposed to be made of glass. I'm not even sure that we *can* make these in glass. Even if we can, tooling up will cost us a fortune." From the clutter on the desk he produced a glass clam, a hand-blown protytpe. "Here, look at this one," he said.

He handed the clam to Larry, who examined it closely, racking his brain for something to say about it.

Edgar Peters waited for a bit, expecting that his son would have something to say. When the silence had grown embarrassing, Mr. Peters cleared his throat and spoke. "First, will anyone buy a glass clam? I doubt that clams have widespread appeal. Second, look at how complex this is: the valves are actually hinged. Look at this! A glass hinge." He snatched the clam from Larry and flipped it open, impatiently, breaking the glass hinge. "Can you imagine what these are going to have to sell for? Well, enough of my worries; tell me what you've been up to."

8

THE READER could be sure, at the beginning of any Larry Peters book, that Larry would soon be up to something interesting, for Larry shared his father's ingenuity for creating amusing diversions, devising interesting

endeavors. Often, these were obviously deriva-
tive: after his father suggested building a raft to
chart the Gulf Stream, Larry suggested casting
adrift bottles containing questionnaires about the
weather conditions and curious local customs of
the areas in which they would eventually wash
ashore; inspired by his father's car-rocking idea,
Larry developed the "dry land sailboat," a dinghy on a platform decorated with a cardboard
sea, which would fit within one half of a two-car
garage and could be rocked by a near relative of
the mechanism his father had designed to rock
automobiles. (The "dry land sailboat" was the
basis for the subplot in *The Thief of Time*. In that
book, Larry entertained hopes that he and Rocky
might go into business for themselves with this
device, but, sadly, their hopes were shattered
when Harrison Whitehead, one of the world's
most distinguished brummagem designers, a
mainstay of the Peters outfit, was killed during
the testing of the prototype when the mock-up
two-car garage filled with real exhaust fumes
from the real car that Larry and Rocky and
Lucinda had brought over from the mainland to
drive the mechanism. The incident was reported
in the Murky Bay *Daily News* under the headline,
"Boating Accident Leaves One Dead.") Others of
Larry's projects were more original: his planting
most of the island in bamboo and hacking out
intricate pathways through it (in *Bamboozled!*)

remains my favorite, and I remember with fond admiration his success in persuading Lucinda and several of her pubescent friends to dye their hair auburn and participate in a *tableau vivant* based on John William Waterhouse's "Hylas and the Nymphs" (in *That Crazy Redhead*).

In each of the Larry Peters adventures, the plot of the adventure itself turned somehow on the latest of Mr. Peters's or Larry's inventions, preoccupations, or avocations. For a reader who was familiar with the series and its conventions, one of the pleasures of reading any new volume came from trying to anticipate the way in which Larry's current interest would figure in the resolution of the mystery, the capture of the crooks, the unmasking of the spies, the rescue of the hostages, or whatever other satisfactory resolution would conclude the story. Take, as an example, *The Phantom Island*, the eleventh novel in the series. In the first chapter, Larry assembles his family in the living room for the unveiling of a painting that he has executed on one of the living-room windows.

> "Well, let's have a look at it," said Edgar Peters, with furrowed brow. He threw a protective arm across the shoulders of his wife, Antonia.
>
> Larry arranged his family in a semicircle facing the draped window. Hector, an old mustard-

CALL ME LARRY • 43

colored dog, followed feebly after them, made his way to a spot just in front of the drapes, groaned, and fell to the floor.

Mrs. Peters spotted some spatters of paint on the rug. She gave a weary sigh. "Oh, Larry, why must these projects always make messes of one sort or another?" she asked.

"Don't worry, Mom," Larry said impatiently. "I'll clean it up. I promise. Lucy, will you do the honors? Just pull the cord over there, and the drapes will part."

Lucinda fumbled around behind the drapes until she found the cord. She struck a pose of some dignity and tugged gently; the drapes began to open but stopped after an inch or two. She gave a less gentle tug. "Something's jammed," she muttered. She wrapped the cord around her hand and gave a vigorous yank, and the entire assembly tore loose from the wall and fell to the floor at her feet, along with some plaster. "Darn it!" she cried, leaping out of the way. When she stepped on his tail, Hector, the old mustard-colored dog, howled and began to struggle to his feet, whimpering.

"Oh, Heck," wailed Lucy. "Did I step on you? I'm sorry."

She reached down to comfort the old fellow, her tiny shorts riding up to expose an eyecatching crescent of the smoothly rounded underside of her tight pubescent buttocks as she did so.

Larry indicated the painted window with a flip of his hand. *"Voila!"* he said.

Mr. Peters cleared his throat. It often occurred to him that if it wasn't one thing it was another; if a radiator wasn't leaking, for example, the pear tree was dying. A little sigh escaped from Mrs. Peters. Hector whimpered and fell to the floor again, rolling over on his back so that Lucinda could scratch his flabby belly, but her attention had returned to the painting.

"It's very—creative," Mrs. Peters said haltingly. "Very creative. It must be wonderful to be able to come up with these ideas."

"It's intended to keep the mind alive," said Larry. "Say you walk into the living room, full of the cares of the workaday world, and you glance out the window." He demonstrated. "Before, you would have seen a familiar view that offered you no escape from your own tedious life because there was nothing interesting in it."

"You're telling me," muttered Lucy.

Mr. Peters shook his head and stared at his shoes. He wondered why young people were so easily bored with life and what he might do to stir up some new excitement.

"Before," said Larry, "you would have seen nothing but the gray waters of Murky Bay. But now you see something interesting, and you have a whole flock of things to wonder about." He began suggesting questions, indicating details in the painting as he did so. "What island is that? How did it get there? Who built the hotel? Why would anyone build a hotel on a little island like that? Why was it abandoned? Is anyone living there now? If so, who? And what about that rowboat, that sunken rowboat at the end of the dilapidated dock?"

I read this passage for the first time with a pleasure that only Larry Peters initiates could share, for my familiarity with the conventions of the series led me at once to the conclusion that this painting would in some way offer a clue to the mystery that was going to unfold as the novel progressed, that this was one of the conventional problems in a Larry Peters story, one of the formal elements that shaped a Larry Peters story, and this knowledge made me feel that I was a participant in the unfolding of that story. A hundred pages or so later, my anticipation was rewarded.

Rocky rolled onto the grass and let out a long sigh. "All right, all right," he said. "Have it your way."

"Oh, Rocky," said Lucinda, "it's not that I don't want to—it's just that I'm afraid I'll get pregnant."

"I told you, Lucy," said Rocky. "You don't have to worry about that if the moon is full. Jeez, you've got me all frustrated now."

Lucinda sat up and rested her head on Rocky's shoulder. Her heart pounded with fear and desire. "Oh, heck," she thought. "Why don't I just let him? The moon sure is full. Whenever it peeks through the clouds it lights up that oval island out there as if it were daytime." She ran her tongue into Rocky's ear, and she rubbed her hand across his chest. He held her head with one strong hand and kissed her, thrusting his tongue deeply, violently, into her mouth. With his other hand he tore her shorts open and reached inside, his fingers probing roughly, poking and prying. Lucinda's eyes opened wide with surprise, with the shock of an unexpected pleasure, and in the moonlight the oval island seemed to flash like the silver underbelly of a gigantic flatfish. All at once Lucinda was struck by the realization that something was very wrong.

"Rocky!" she shouted, pushing herself away from him and wriggling from his grasp.

"Oh, God, what is it now?" moaned Rocky.

"That island!" she cried.

"What about it?" wailed Rocky, striking the grass repeatedly with his fists.

"It's coming closer!"

Rocky leaped to his feet and peered out over the Bay. There was no doubt about it. In the moonlight, he could see a wake behind the island. The entire island was moving toward them, and it was moving fast.

"Come on," he said. "We've got to get help!"

9

LARRY'S MOTHER was entire-
ly occupied with domestic affairs, although she
didn't actually do much work. Marie did most of
the cooking, though Mrs. Peters had several
dishes for which she was famous: her chow-chow
relish, piccalilli, one-eyed Egyptians, hoppin'
John, and pigs-in-blankets were family favorites.
Marie made the beds, did the laundry, ordered
supplies for delivery from Murky Bay, and gener-
ally bustled around, wisecracking, pushing dust
around, and offering down-to-earth advice;
employees of the knickknack works did the heavier maintenance work. Mrs. Peters was the
domestic manager. She organized everything. It
was clear to me from the start that although there
was a surface dottiness to her character, she made
everything in the Peters ménage work. None of
the Peterses could be described as level-headed,
but Antonia Peters possessed the levelest of the
Peters heads; she was the only member of the
Peters family who could be counted on, when six
or seven things were happening at once, to pick
out the one thing that most needed immediate
attention. Consider the situation in *The Camel's
Back*. One morning, after Lucinda has brought

the workers from shore to the island on the Peters barge, a resounding crash, coming from who-knows-where on the island, rattles the windows in the big old Peters house. At that moment, the family is gathered in the dining room, eating breakfast.

"My goodness!" cried Mrs. Peters. "What was that?"

"It was a crash of some kind," said Larry. "Would you pass me the sausages, Dad?"

"Do you think it might have been serious?" asked Mrs. Peters.

"Oh, I doubt it, dear," said Edgar Peters. He put his fork down and reached for a platter of link sausages. He stopped before actually raising the platter, however. "Did you want the link sausages, Larry, or the sausage patties?" he asked.

"Gee, I'm not sure," said Larry. "What kind are you having, Sexpot?" he asked Lucinda in the wisecracking tone that brother and sister used with each other.

"I'm going to have one of those cute little links," she replied saucily. "They're just about the size of your—"

"I think we should investigate," said Mrs. Peters. Her brow was furrowed with concern.

"I haven't had any complaints yet, Green Eyes," Larry asserted cockily, passing the platter of link sausages to his sister.

"Stop teasing, you two," said Edgar Peters in

the kindly tone he always used with his son and daughter. "Antonia," he said to his wife, in the reassuring tone he often employed when speaking with her, "I'm sure that if anything serious has occurred, my brother Hector will be here shortly to tell us all about it."

"The only reason Larry hasn't had any complaints," said a tall, handsome young man who suddenly stepped through the doorway to the dining room, "is that he hasn't had any customers."

"Rocky!" squealed Lucinda. She leaped from her chair, upsetting her glass of prune juice, and ran to Rocky. She threw herself at the smiling young man, winding her arms around his neck and her long, honey-colored legs around his waist. She began covering his face with kisses.

"Hey, take it easy, Hot Stuff," said Rocky, cupping her tight pubescent buttocks in his large and muscular hands. "I've had a long, hard night."

"Did you learn anything about that swarthy stranger, Rocky?" asked Edgar Peters, in the sober tone he employed when there was a problem to be solved.

"Dear," said Antonia Peters, "I really think that before we do anything else we ought to investigate that crash." There was a petulant tone in her voice, which Edgar Peters interpreted as meaning that she felt she was being ignored.

"Now, dear," he began, thinking that it might be best to humor her and investigate the crash, so that they could get on to more important things.

"Hey, I heard that too," said Rocky. With Lucinda still wrapped around him, he made his way to the sideboard, where he took a piece of raisin-bread toast from a silver toast caddy. "There was a lot of dust and debris falling out of the air in the vicinity of the design building." He winked at Larry and said, "I figured it was one of your projects, Larry."

"I really think that we—" began Antonia Peters, but just then Hector Peters, Edgar Peters's brother, burst into the dining room, dragging behind him, covered with dust from head to toe, Ignatz Steinmetz, the brilliant European gewgaw designer who had become, in two short years, one of the most valuable members of the Peters team.

"Edgar!" cried Hector. "We're ruined!"

"There you are, Antonia," said Edgar Peters, reaching out to pat his wife's hand in a reassuring manner. "I told you that if the crash was serious Hector would soon be here to tell us about it." He turned to his brother, his eyebrows knit in a look of grave concern. "It's serious then, Hector?" he asked.

"Steinmetz," said Hector Peters, "tell him what you told me."

"Ruins!" cried the world-renowned designer. "Everything is in ruins!" When he gesticulated, and he gesticulated extravagantly, dust flew from his laboratory coat. His left cheek was badly scraped, and his hands were trembling. "We were working on the new models, and Entwhistle said, 'How about a cup of coffee, Iggie?' and I said, 'Sure, why not?' and then kerwhammy! The roof falls in and the whole place is a shambles!"

10

LARRY'S SISTER, Lucinda, was as cute as a button and smart as a whip. She and Larry loved trading wisecracks; in fact, I realize, reflecting on the Peterses now and bringing to mind my feelings toward them when I was a boy, that the wisecracking and playful teasing among them was meant to serve as a sign of the love that they felt for one another, something I didn't understand at the time. To me then, it seemed no more than a part of their exciting and unpredictable style, but even if I considered it no more than an element of style, the wisecracking was one of those constants of the Peters household that persisted beyond the adventures, and was therefore one of the truly valuable aspects of the books and of life in the Peters family. There was little wisecracking in my family, and I came to think that there would be a good deal more fun and immeasurably more panache if only there were more wisecracking. The Peterses' wisecracking seemed to be one of the few things that I might translate from Larry's life into mine.

"Peter," said my father one morning while I was musing along the foregoing lines, "would you bring me an ash tray?"

"Ash and ye shall reshieve," I said.

My father gave me a pained look, and I came quickly to the conclusion that there are, essentially, two kinds of families, wisecracking families and non-wisecracking families, and that it had been my unfortunate lot to be born into one of the latter.

Whenever Lucinda entered a scene, I began to smile as I read, for I knew that something interesting was going to happen. She was a year younger than Larry, but since girls mature more quickly than boys, she easily held her own in their amiable tussles, both verbal and physical. (The ages of the characters in the Larry Peters adventures were never given. The only references to age that I can recall were relative: we were told somewhere in one of the early books that Lucinda was a year younger than Larry and that Rocky was three years older. After considerable reading in the literature, I've concluded that Lucinda and Larry, given the different rates at which they matured, were both somewhere in late-early to early-middle adolescence and that Rocky was just post-adolescent.)

Lucinda's character was wildly variable. She'd act like one of the guys at one time, grow shy and retiring at another, become brazen and sarcastic, headstrong, cautious, and who-knows-what-all by turns. Her appearance was never described in full, and even the fragments that the reader was given now and then, glimpses, as it were, through a curtain parted by a puff of a summer night's breeze, were vague, more tantalizing than satisfying. This vagueness was, I concluded, deliberate and wise, since the reader was, thanks to the lack of details about her appearance, allowed, even encouraged, to construct his own Lucinda from bits and pieces of girls he knew, or a girl he had merely glimpsed—at the beach, say, dropping a strap of her bathing suit down over her arm, rubbing sun-tan lotion onto her shoulder absent-mindedly while she stared out across the surf toward the shimmering horizon, or stretched out on the foredeck of a lean blue sloop, wearing red-rimmed reflective sunglasses, reading a paper-back book the title of which one could not make out, or perhaps perched with a group of friends on the varnished handrail atop the railing that ran along the boardwalk, raising her right leg to scratch, just at the edge of the line imprinted by the elastic of her bathing suit, the irregular red welt of a horsefly bite—for these books were in one respect truly masterful pieces of work: they provided a context for the fantasies of adolescent boys, a context so reassuring that the timidity and fear that ordinarily attended those fantasies nearly disappeared when they were entertained within it. One's parents and other adults, who seemed at times to be regarding one with lancet eyes, eyes that penetrated straight to that abscess where one's guilty urges matured, did not go to Kittiwake Island.

If the bond between Larry and Rocky became for me the paradigm of friendship, and it did, what existed between Larry and Lucy made me wish for that special relationship that can exist only between a brother and sister. What is it that makes that relationship what it is? It is, I suppose, partly narcissistic. Here is an interlocutor who understands all your references, who shares your habits of speech, who even sounds a bit like you. Here is a girl who reminds you of yourself. Here is your companion, if your ages are close, as Lucy's and Larry's were, in growing up. I didn't have to envy Larry for his having Rocky, the older male friend, who had seen so much more of the world than Larry had, who could teach him the things that a worldly older male friend can, since I had Raskolnikov, who showed every sign of growing up to be a lot like Rocky, but I envied Larry very much for his having Lucinda, the younger sister, together with whom he was able to learn so much by trial and error, as was the case in *No Laughing Matter.*

"What was that?" whispered Larry.

"I didn't hear anything," said Lucinda.

"I think someone's coming," said Larry. "I'm sure I heard someone laugh out there in the dark." He switched his flashlight off. He and Lucinda stood silently in the darkness.

"I don't hear anything," said Lucinda.

"I'm sure now," said Larry. "I heard someone laugh, and I heard footsteps, the footsteps of two people, two heavy people, on the gravel outside." Larry took Lucinda's hand and squeezed it. "We've got to hide," he said. "I wish I could remember where that ladder was. We could hide in the hayloft above us if we could find the ladder, but I'm afraid we might miss our footing in the dark and make a noise. If only I could risk turning the flashlight on for an instant. Wait a minute! There was a wooden box of some kind around here, wasn't there?"

"Larry, are you sure someone's out there? I didn't hear anything," said Lucinda.

"Lucy," whispered Larry. "I've found the box! Hurry! Climb in here. If they find us, there's no telling what they'll do to us!"

The urgency in her brother's voice was clear. Lucy moved quickly and soundlessly to the box and climbed inside while he held the lid open. The box was narrow and shallow, just about the right size, Lucy reflected as she climbed in, for a coffin. The thought sent a shiver down her spine. She stretched out in the box and Larry climbed in and lowered the lid.

"There's not much room in here," said Larry. "I don't think I can squeeze beside you. I'm going to have to lie on top of you."

"That's okay," whispered Lucinda. "It's pretty comfortable. Somebody has put a blanket and pillow in here."

"That's a stroke of good luck," said Larry.

"Hey, what are you doing?" asked Lucinda.

"I'm just trying to find a comfortable position," said Larry.

"If you make yourself any more comfortable, we're going to have to get engaged," said Lucinda.

Larry stifled a laugh. He and Lucinda loved trading wisecracks like this.

"It's pretty hot in here, isn't it?" said Larry.

"It sure is," said Lucinda. "What are you doing now?"

"I'm just trying to get these hot clothes off."

"Larry, let me out of here!"

"It's not safe out there, Sis."

"It's not safe in here either, Brother."

11

MARIE, the Peterses' maid, made my heart go pit-a-pat the moment she first appeared in one of the adventures, pushing the kitchen door open with a beautifully rounded hip, stepping into the dining room on those long and luscious legs, carrying a tray of blueberry pancakes, just as, I'm sure, she made the hearts of most of the boys who read the Larry Peters books beat faster whenever she appeared. Marie never figured very prominently in the adventures themselves, though she would pop in now and then; ordinarily, she was left at home when the pace of the action picked up, and we wouldn't see her again until the end of the book, when the adventurers—tired, possibly injured, but always victorious—returned to Kittiwake Island and sat down to another big meal. Most of my ideas about Marie came from outside the books themselves, from other sources and from my imagination. There were, however, one or two scenes in which Marie appeared that have remained sharp and clear and brilliant in my memory. I am willing to bet a sizable sum that any reader of the Larry Peters books will recall one of those scenes immediately and vividly if I merely end this sentence with the phrase *tub of Jell-O.*

In *The Flying Aspidistras,* Kittiwake Island is invaded by a squadron of thugs and goons in the pay of an evil manufacturer of rubber houseplants who is planning to move into the gewgaw business, and Marie and Larry are bound hand and foot and set adrift in a leaking rowboat. As the water in the rowboat rises, and Larry and Marie confront the likelihood that the next few minutes will be their last, Marie tells Larry that what makes her saddest is the thought of the many things she hoped to do in the life that she had imagined still stretched out before her like a long highway, with mysterious stretches hidden behind curves or over hills, with forks and crossroads where she might have, on impulse, veered from the broad, well-traveled way and so on.

> "Well," said Larry, "I guess that road into the future has come to a dead end." He laughed bitterly, and then his voice softened. "I'm sorry that you won't get to do all those things, Marie," he said gently.
>
> "So am I," said Marie. Her voice caught, a shudder ran through her, and she swallowed hard.
>
> "Say," said Larry, forcing a lighthearted tone into his voice, "suppose you could do just one of those things. What would it be?"

"One?" asked Marie. "Oh, my goodness. One? I don't know, I—"

"What's the first one that pops into your head?"

"Oh, well," said Marie. "The first one that pops into my head? I—oh, I don't know—I—well—I've always thought it would be fun to—you know that big claw-foot tub in my bathroom?"

"Sure," said Larry. He blushed as soon as he had spoken, for he had on many an evening climbed the apple tree outside the window of Marie's bathroom in the hope of catching a glimpse of her while she bathed in the claw-foot tub to which she referred, and had, in fact, succeeded on a number of occasions.

"Well, I've often thought that it would be fun to draw a nice hot bath in that tub and then stir in—oh, you'll laugh at me."

"No, Marie, I won't," said Larry. There was so much genuine compassion in his voice that Marie was able to continue without embarrassment.

"Well," she said, "I'd stir in about—oh, I guess, two or three dozen packages of Jell-O."

"Jell-O?" asked Larry. His heart had begun to beat at a faster rate.

"What's your favorite flavor?" asked Marie.

"Raspberry," said Larry, in a hoarse whisper.

"I'd stir in all that raspberry Jell-O and then slip off my nightgown and settle into the tub."

"Oh my God," said Larry. His heart beat pit-a-pat.

"I'd rest my head on the edge of the tub and lie there in the warm water and just relax while the water cooled and the Jell-O firmed around me—"

"Oh," said Larry. "Pit-a-pat, pit-a-pat," said his heart.

"—shaping itself to every inch of me—"

"Ah," said Larry. His heart was beating now with a small, sharp pain, as if a thorn had lodged in it.

"—and perhaps I'd fall asleep. When I woke up, I'd be enveloped by Jell-O, snug in a tub of Jell-O, resilient raspberry Jell-O, molded to me, embracing me as no lover ever could, as not even a hundred lovers could embrace me at once."

A sound something like a sob came from Larry.

"And then, very softly, I would call out, 'Help. Help me, Larry.' "

"What?" asked Larry. "What?"

"And you would open the door of the bathroom—"

"I would?"

"—and you'd be holding—now, don't laugh—"

"What would I be holding? What?"

"A spoon."

"A spoon. Oh, my God, a spoon."

"Not a big spoon. A little spoon, a demitasse spoon."

12

I THINK that most readers of the Larry Peters books dreamed of being a friend of Larry's, of being found washed up on Kittiwake Island one morning, carried to the big house on an improvised litter, nursed back to health by Marie and Mrs. Peters, and then adopted into the Peters circle. The attitude inspired in me by the Larry Peters books was fundamentally different. I didn't want to be *like* Larry Peters; I wanted to *be* Larry Peters. I wanted his chum Rocky King to be my chum on exactly the terms that existed between him and Larry. I wanted his brilliant and unpredictable dad to be my dad. I wanted his fussy, cuddly mother to be my mother. I wanted Marie to turn down my sheets. I wanted to sit up at night, after everyone else was asleep, and trade confidences and wisecracks with my saucy sister Lucy. I knew that this was, in all the ways that most people would have considered important, impossible. But I understood even then that there were ways in which it was not only possible but necessary, necessary in a way that only the things we truly want to do, truly derive pleasure from doing, are necessary, however complex and demanding they may be. If

Roger Drake had been able to imagine Larry and all the rest of them and the context for them, surely I could manage to imagine myself as Larry, could imagine a complete and consistent enough set of details to fill the chinks in Mr. Drake's portrait of Larry with details about myself, to have Larry say what I would say during the breakfast conversations on the mornings when there was no adventure to interrupt, when the Peterses could stretch out and relax, putter in the garden, read the papers, listen to a record, play the piano, go for a swim.

I spent a lot of time within the Larry Peters books, playing at being Larry, but I never thought of myself as escaping into them, never thought of myself as retreating into them to get away from a world that wasn't what it ought to have been, never thought of myself as making my way across Murky Bay in the hope of finding something better or leaving something worse behind, never, that is, until my great-grandmother died.

13

GREAT-GRANDMOTHER Leroy was ill for months, but I didn't realize how seriously ill she was until Grandfather moved her downstairs from her rooms in the attic. She moved into the room across the hall from what had been my father's bedroom when he was a boy and was now the bedroom I used when I visited. She never left the bed. For several weeks before she died, she didn't speak. Sometimes when I visited, I sat beside her bed for an hour or so and talked without even pausing for a response. I knew that she wasn't going to say anything, so I just talked on and on, quicker and quicker, to keep the silence from settling over her like a shroud. When I ran out of events that had occurred at school, episodes that had passed with my playmates, things I had learned, and things I had heard or seen, I recounted for her episodes from the Larry Peters books, and when I came to those gaps between scenes, between chapters, when the action in one chapter ended and the action of the next, set somewhere else, hadn't yet begun, I filled those gaps, as, years earlier, I had filled the gaps in my understanding of the Leroy family history when I had recited it for Great-

grandmother in her attic rooms, with sawdust—
that is, with episodes that I made up on my own,
as one uses sawdust to fill the cracks in the
bottom of a wooden boat. Throughout all my
chatter, Great-grandmother never said a thing.

But then, one afternoon, Great-grandmother
suddenly interrupted me, as if she had heard
enough at last. I was startled by her voice. I
hadn't expected to hear her talk at all, but I must
have had in the back of my mind the idea that if
she were to speak, her voice would be as thin and
tired as her face had become. Instead, it was
nearly as strong as it had always been, and it
deceived me into thinking that she had suddenly
gotten better.

"Peter," she said. "I have a present for you."

"You do?" I glanced around the room. "Where
is it?" I asked.

"Upstairs," she said. "You go up and get it."

I went upstairs and opened the glass door to
her rooms. Something strange had happened to
these rooms while she had been out of them. Left
alone, the things there had begun to claim owner-
ship. The chair where Great-grandmother used to
sit and carve coconuts to represent Leroys had
become the strongest personality in the room
now, and it sat in command, dark and heavy, in
front of the windows, silhouetted against the
curtained light. I looked around, but for a while I
couldn't find anything that looked like a present.

Then, on one of the shelves that held the coconuts, I saw a box, nearly cubical. The box wasn't
wrapped, or even tied with ribbon, but it was
taped shut, and when I took it from the shelf, I
found, written on the top, in pencil, the words
FOR PETER.

From the heft and size, I was certain that the
box held a coconut. A lump formed in my throat,
and tears filled my eyes. I decided at once that
Great-grandmother had carved a coconut to represent herself, and that by giving it to me she was
telling me that she expected to die. I lifted the lid
gravely, slowly, holding my hands symmetrically,
palms parallel, fingers extended, raising the lid
directly upward and slowly setting it down to one
side, for I had begun to serve as an altar boy at
the Babbington Episcopal Church and had developed an exaggerated sense of ceremony. Great-
grandmother's coconut heads looked so like one
another, and I was so completely prepared to
find one carved in Great-grandmother's likeness
and to feel grief at the sight of it, that for a
moment or two I didn't recognize that the coconut represented me. Not only had Great-grandmother carved the coconut in my likeness, but
she had carved me laughing, though the faces of
the other Leroys were tight-lipped and stern. I
hurried downstairs, smiling.

Great-grandmother was chuckling when I

came into the bedroom. "I always meant to get around to you," she said.

"Thanks, Grandma," I said. "Is it all right if I take it home with me?"

"Of course it's all right, Peter," she said. "You can have all of them."

This gift brought with it a pleasure so buoyant that it was dizzying, almost frightening. I kissed Great-grandmother, and as soon as I left the room where she lay I could feel the lightness of my delight lifting me from the floor, feel myself drifting upward as easily as a soaring bird, up the stairs to her room, where I spent the rest of the afternoon drifting on the air there, so dense with memories and dust, and playing with my heads.

When I came downstairs much later, with the head of Black Jacques under my left arm and my own under my right, the door to the room where Great-grandmother lay was locked, and my parents were in the living room with Grandfather and Grandmother, making plans for the funeral.

That night I lay in bed, wakeful and anxious and hurt. Everything seemed wrong. Everything seemed confused. My thoughts were turbid, roiling, like wrack stirred up by a storm. I couldn't make sense of them, and I couldn't drive them away. Then, at last, I saw through the murk a heartening yellow light, and after a while I could see that it was coming from the windows of the Peterses' living room, where everyone was gathered to trade wisecracks after dinner, where no one good was going to die, where things were as they ought to be; and since there was a rowboat handy, I stepped into it, shoved off, and began rowing. With each stroke my arms grew more tired, heavier, my mad and disappointing world receded, and from Kittiwake Island I could hear Lucinda calling me, calling me to come in now, to come in off Murky Bay and join them in the living room, and she was calling me Larry.

14

SOME EIGHT YEARS later, on a cold February afternoon during my sophomore year at Hargrove University, I sat in Cranston Library, trying to study for a mathematics examination. The library was overheated; I was sitting in an overstuffed leather wing chair, the type of chair that I have, ever since my days at Hargrove, thought of as the only type of chair proper for a library. Snow was falling outside, and the air in the library was heavy with the odor of wet wool, wet leather, old books, painted steam radiators, and students, many of us dozing over our studies. I stretched, yawned, and decided to take a break from my work to read a letter from a high school acquaintance, Robert Meyer, a boy who had passed through Babbington High School almost unnoticed, but who had this year done a daring thing for that time, taken a year's sabbatical from college to be on his own in Europe. As soon as he reached European soil, Robert had begun writing to everyone who had ignored him in high school. He wrote long, tedious letters, letters full of strained insights, accounts of unlikely sexual encounters, and snatches of the local language. I received at least one a week. When the first of his letters arrived, I had no idea who Robert Meyer was, and it wasn't until I began hearing from friends who had also received letters from him that I was able to retrieve a blurry face from my memory of high school, someone rushing past in the hallway, mumbling a greeting, but averting his face and hurrying on, someone still sitting in the stands after a football game, alone, at one end of the upper row of bleachers, while the rest of us headed for the gate, the parking lot, cars, pizza. I looked him up in my yearbook, but his photograph was no more help to me in recalling Robert just a year after we had been in school together than the photographs of my other classmates would be twenty-five years later. Though I was happy to receive any mail, even letters from Robert, they grew wearying after a while, and so when one arrived I delayed opening it for a little longer than I had delayed opening the last. This one had been in my bookbag for several days. I tore open the thin blue envelope, unfolded the letter and read.

"Ich bin nun endlich in München und sitze hier in meinem Zimmer bei Frau Brenner in der Schellingstrasse," the letter began. The heat, the odors, and Robert Meyer's prose style put me to sleep nearly at once. I had been sitting with my feet up on a table, and I had leaned backward in the chair until it rocked on the back legs only. When I woke, I was sitting on a dilapidated wooden dock, the sort of dock from which you are certain to pick up splinters in your feet if you walk along it barefoot. Rusty nailheads projected from pilings where boards had once been attached. Other boards, half rotted, hung at odd angles. Beside the dock was a rowboat, a sunken rowboat, resting on the sandy bottom in a foot or so of water. An old line, green with slime, still made the rowboat fast to a piling at the end of the dock. I was barefoot, and I was playing a game with the surface of the water—the same game that I used to play when I let my feet dangle over the stern of the *Rambunctious,* Big Grandfather's boat—I was trying to bring the soles of my feet as close to the surface of the water as I could without touching it. It was day, but the day was foggy; it was summer, and I was wearing only a pair of shorts and a short-sleeved shirt. A wavelet

touched my heel, and I kicked my feet and ran my toes through the water. It was still and warm. I was nine or ten.

Faintly, I began to hear something through the fog; as the sound grew stronger, I thought I recognized it, but I couldn't be quite sure: it might be only the lapping of waves, but the water was still; it might be laughter, but who would be out in the fog, laughing?

"Are you all right?" A young woman with dark hair stepped out of the fog and brought her face near mine. I found myself sitting straight in a leather chair, my back pressed firmly along its back, my legs flat along the seat where the dock ought to have been, my lower legs against the edge of the cushion, and from around me I heard a sound that I thought I recognized, a sound that might be laughter, but I saw no people; a sound that might be the lapping of waves, if there were waves inside a building. Certainly I was inside a building, but I was looking at the ceiling, and if the evidence of my eyes was to be believed, the ceiling had been moved around to occupy the plane ordinarily occupied by a wall. Some sort of practical joke? Not likely, I thought. A trick of the mind, the not-quite-fully-awake mind. Transpositions of this sort were, I knew from my several attempts to read *A La Recherche du Temps Perdu*, not uncommon illusions upon awakening; in the misty margin between sleep and wakefulness Marcel might seem to recognize the architecture and furnishings of his room at home, only to find that soon the uplifted forefinger of day had rearranged the furniture, the windows, the doorways, and the walls, to transform his bedroom into a hotel room with a view of the sea.

(Since it has occurred to me just now and is such a fine illustration of the fundamental truths one sometimes finds in fiction, I will mention briefly an anecdote that Porky White told me many years later. He and his wife, Marcella, had traveled to a small lakeside village somewhere in New England for a wedding. The ceremony was intimate and touching, and the party that followed was long and exuberant. Porky retired in wonderful spirits, more than a little soused. "In the middle of the night," he told me, "I get a message from my unconscious: 'Porky! Wake up! You have got to take a piss, and you have got to do it right now,' it was saying. Quiet as I can be, I get out of bed, step out of the bedroom into the dark hallway, turn right, turn right again into the bathroom, walk to the toilet, reach into my shorts and pull out my pride and joy, yawn, and let myself go. Instead of the basso splashing I usually hear under these circumstances, I hear an odd, hollow, splattering sound, and this incongruity wakes me up. I'm not in my own house, of course, I'm not in my bathroom, and I'm pissing onto the caned seat of a fine old bentwood chair.")

"Oh, sure," I said to the young woman with dark hair. "I'm fine. I just dozed off." I yawned and stretched and rubbed my eyes. I thought that some fresh air might be in order, and I tried to get up. Only then, when my body told me that gravity was pulling from the wrong direction, did I realize that the chair and I were lying on our backs on the floor, and that the laughter was real, directed at me. I scrambled to my feet, righted the chair, stacked my books and papers, trying not to raise my head all the while, so that I wouldn't have to see any of the people who were laughing at me. I made my way, with what I hoped was dignified haste, through the doors of the main entrance and out into the bright sunlight. The sun was so bright after the library that I closed my eyes against it for a moment and reeled with a dazzled dizziness. In the iridescent images in my mind's eye I saw a piece of a persistent memory of part of a dream, no more than a snapshot, but a clear and intriguing snapshot: that moment of sitting on the old dock.

15

AS TIME PASSED, the snap-
shot stayed in my mind. I could recover the
picture of myself sitting on the dock whenever I
wished, just by closing my eyes and willing it to
appear. I assumed that it was a memory, but,
unlike most memories, the picture became clearer
with time, more detailed, more precise. I could
feel my sensations better, more clearly, as time
passed. At the same time, however, much about
this memory made little sense to me, and expla-
nations eluded me. Where was I? How did I get
there? I had my suspicions. My maternal grandmother, Gumma, was a believer in recurring
dreams that passed from generation to generation, dreams that arose from acts of such power
that they inspired emotions too strong to die in a
single lifetime. She claimed to have one herself, a
dream about rushing along a curving corridor,
opening a series of doors, and falling after she
opened the last one. She was convinced that this
derived from something terrible that her grandmother had done. My mother had one, one that I
didn't know about until I told her, years before,
about a dream that I had had while I tossed
restlessly during a bout with one of the childhood

diseases, something that made me feverish. It was a dream in which nothing happened. There was a featureless landscape; it might have been a desert or tundra. In the foreground was a post, and from the post a line of some kind dangled. The post, and, even more than the post, the line dangling from it, made me feel miserable, nauseated, frightened, horribly empty, as if something terrible had happened and things would never be right again. When I told my mother about this, I did so reluctantly, because during this restless and feverish time I had, by assembling in a careful, step-by-step, logical fashion the few facts I knew, the rumors, assertions, wild claims, and flights of fancy I had heard, and the mystifying hints in a pamphlet my mother had left in my room, arrived at a clear theoretical understanding—which in form resembled the instruction sheets that came with the model airplanes I had become fond of building, an insert-part-A-into-part-B understanding—of what men and women did when they "went to bed together," and had discovered, by way of looking for an experimental method to test my theory, masturbation. I had a hunch that my unsettling dream might have something to do with that.

"Oh, Peter," said my mother. "I have that dream too."

"You do?" I asked.

"Oh, yes. But I know why."

"I think I know why too," I said, looking at my hands.

"It's because of the rowboat."

"The rowboat?"

She explained a painful memory. One Sunday when she was a little girl, Gumma and Guppa had organized a picnic on one of the islands in the Bay. Friends had traveled to the island in boats, and after a while the children had wandered away from the adults to amuse themselves. The amusement for the youngest children consisted of throwing sand and pebbles into a dinghy that Garth and May Castle had used to row from their sloop to the island. The rowboat was tied to a piece of driftwood that the Castles had thrust into the sand. In time, the children succeeded in sinking the dinghy, and they cheered when it settled to the bottom. When it was discovered, none of the adults had been particularly angry, in fact most had thought the incident funny, but my mother had felt ashamed of her part in the business, and she insisted that a sudden wind had arisen and blown the sand and pebbles into the dinghy while the children watched, helpless and aghast. As time passed, she became more ashamed of the lie than of the act it was meant to hide. She thought that the recurring dream showed the piece of driftwood and the line leading into the water. I thought for a while that my sitting-on-the-dock memory might have been a more precise version of that dream returned to trouble me again, but I have never been a believer in such things, so I continued to look for another explanation.

I thought that the dock might be on Small's Island. But things were not quite right. For one thing, I was not quite myself in this scene; for another, the island was not quite Small's Island. I was reminded of the eerie feeling Raskol described so many years before, when he told the Glynns and me about his crawling through a culvert into what he took to be another world. Finally, with all the force of the truth, the explanation hit me. I was in this snapshot the young Larry Peters, but not quite the young Larry Peters with whom I was familiar. I was the young Larry Peters as he would have been if I had been the young Larry Peters. I was Larry Peters before the adventures began, before the family had prospered, when Larry's father was still struggling to make his gewgaw business go. Something else struck me at nearly the same time. The picture of myself as the young Larry Peters that I had in my mind was becoming clearer with time because it was not a memory, because I was making it up.

16

MY ABILITY to imagine my-
self as Larry Peters improved with time, and I
must admit that I used it now and then to get
away. And I have continued to do so. I'm just old
enough now—as I write these words I am forty
years and thirty-eight days old—to be able to
admit without embarrassment that I never really
abandoned most of my childhood habits and
interests, certainly not the pleasant pastime of
slipping into the character of Larry Peters.

For several years, while I finished college and
took a master's degree in molluscan biology, my
version of Larry developed without any apparent
assistance from me. He simply sat in that comfortable corner of my mind, on Kittiwake Island,
which came to resemble Small's Island more and
more, and a life grew around him while I
neglected him, as beach grass will grow in sand
under the worst conditions. Whenever I rowed
out to the island to see what he was up to I was
surprised to find how much more I knew about
him, how much more there was to know about
him.

From time to time, I began jotting down my
thoughts about Larry, conversations that he

might have been involved in before the summer
of the adventures, or after that summer, when he
went off to college, or later, when he returned to
the island.

Albertine and I married, and, as most people
who can read do at some time or other, often in
their youth, I began to want to write a book.
And, as most people do who begin to want to
write a book, especially those who begin to want
to write a book in their youth, I wanted to write a
book about myself. Unlike many people who
want to write books about themselves, I was
embarrassed to admit it, even to myself, and so I
cast about for a way to write a book about myself
without seeming to. I didn't know exactly what I
was going to put into this book if I was going to
avoid putting in anything about myself, if I was
not going to admit that it was ego that made me
want to write a book at all, that my only reason
for wanting to write a book was to cry out in an
acceptable way, "Look at me! Over here! Look at
me! Watch this: no hands! See? Wait, wait! Look
at this! I can do it with my eyes closed! Watch!"
Had I simply been willing to admit all that,
however, I would have written, had I managed to
write a book at all, a chaotic, pointless, formless
book, because I hadn't more than the foggiest,
inchoate notion of what I was like. It took nearly
twenty years for me to discover what my books
should be like, and during all that time I wrestled

every day with big, powerful ideas, ideas that were much bigger and stronger than I. How apt that time-worn image for struggling with a big idea is, the image of grappling, grasping, clutching, twisting, trying to hold on to a squirming, powerful, slippery idea that strives to elude you, to get out of your clutches. I wrestled with form and style and tone and argument, and the book grew larger and more diverse, more populous, more anarchic.

What headaches I gave myself over this. What pits of despair I threw myself into. How difficult I was to live with. What a pest I was at parties. More and more often, to get to sleep at night, to escape the big ideas, I would make my way across Murky Bay to trade wisecracks with Rocky and Lucinda and Marie.

17

ONE SUMMER NIGHT, when my struggles had only begun, Albertine and I were sitting on Big Grandfather's front porch. We had been spending the summer with Grandfather, in his house. Grandmother had died during the past year, and our presence in the house was supposed to cheer Grandfather up, to keep the place from echoing with sorrow and loneliness. We felt that we hadn't succeeded, and we had become convinced that we couldn't have succeeded, that we should have known that Grandfather felt the loss of my grandmother too strongly for us to make him forget it for long.

However, of an evening, the three of us would sit on his front porch, on the glider, or in metal chairs that were suspended on springs within metal frames and wheezed when we rocked in them, and I would tell my grandfather stories about things that had happened at work. I was working right down the street, in the boatyard that was once Cap'n Leech's, then Leech's son's, and is now Raskolnikov's. Crazy and amusing things happened there; crazy things happen wherever pleasure boats are moored near working boats, because people who think that boats are for fun and people who think that boats are for work each think the others are crazy. I was a college student at the time, so of course I thought everyone was crazy. My grandfather and Albertine and I would sit and rock and drink gin-and-tonics, and I'd tell my stories, and sometimes I would make Grandfather laugh. When I made him laugh, I'd add to what I had told him, embellish, improvise, mimic, burlesque to make him laugh again, because, after all, I was supposed to try to cheer him up.

On that night, it had grown late, and the three of us had grown quiet. We would be going upstairs to bed soon. Out of the darkness, Grandfather asked me what I wanted to do with myself. I told him what I had told only Albertine before, that I wanted to write a book, and in the confessional safety of the darkness, the security of this familiar setting and sympathetic audience, I felt myself ready to try to tell him all about the book, the impossibly big book, that I wanted to write.

"That's good," he said, before I had a chance to say more. "That's very good. Make sure that there's a laugh on every page."

I stopped myself. I didn't tell him anything about the book I wanted to write. I took a sudden cheap pity on him, who didn't need or want it. I indulged him. I'm not sure now just how I answered him, but I must have said something like, "That's an interesting idea."

And in the darkness I smiled to myself a shameful, condescending smile, and decided that it would be too difficult to explain to Grandfather why I didn't want laughs, why laughing seemed to me reprehensible in this miserable world. In truth, I learned only much later, explaining would have been too difficult because I didn't understand that the main reason that I considered laughter inappropriate was that my circle of serious friends considered it so, walked with their eyes down, their heads bowed by the misery of life. To expect happiness was insane; to want happiness was arrogant and selfish. I had come to regard having a good time, laughing without irony, singing anything but the blues, dancing of any sort as childishly foolish, betrayals of one's unwillingness or inability to face up to the horror that is Life. To indulge in any of the foregoing whoopee, I had to be drunk; but my drinking, even if it led to laughing, singing, and dancing, was not of the variety that makes a young suburban matron, leading her grinning husband to the door, wonder why she wasted the money having her hair done for this terrible night, makes her turn to her hosts and say, "He thinks he has to drink to have a good time. I'm sorry about the tray of glasses"; no, it was the variety that makes a dark-eyed model stub out her Camel and say to her hosts, before she drags the young painter or poet or sculptor or playwright or filmmaker or novelist off, "Only bourbon dulls his pain." I couldn't have explained to Grandfather then that I wanted the respect of all those very serious people, people for whom it was an axiom that no serious thought could lead to laughter, real laughter. And since I couldn't explain, I yawned and said, "Are you ready for bed, Al?"

Albertine and I went up to bed, and when we got in and pulled the sheet over us and lay quietly in the dark, I heard Grandfather on the porch, rocking his chair and making the springs wheeze, tapping his foot, and whistling the tune to "Nagasaki," a ridiculous ditty that, suddenly, loudly, he began to sing:

Hot ginger and dynamite:
That's all there is at night,
Back in Nagasaki
Where the fellas chew tobaccy
And the women wicki-wacki-woooooo—

A neighbor slammed her window down, as she had done on another evening, when Albertine and I had stayed on the porch too late with friends and I had begun to talk too loudly about the nature of things. Grandfather stopped singing, and I heard him come into the house. In a little while, when he came upstairs, I heard him chuckling, and so ignorant was I of the way life really is that I thought his sorrow must have driven him mad. I didn't understand at all that the memories accumulated during years of happiness could weigh enough to balance so large a loss, or that the mind will sometimes find a way to free the heart from pain.

18

ALMOST FOUR YEARS later, Albertine and I were sitting in Mr. Beaker's living room one evening. We had come for dinner, and we had been having a wonderful time. The conversation had been lively, and Eliza genuinely had, I think, enjoyed our youthful volubility. Albertine and I were so full of ourselves and of each other just then that in conversation we never really confronted a subject directly: we could only talk about its relationship to, meaning for, effect on, or even irrelevance to, ourselves.

It was late now, and the four of us had moved from the dining room to the living room, where we sat sipping cognac, which I was trying very hard to learn how to sip, and talking, talking, talking. Mr. Beaker had been, throughout the evening, urging me to take a position that had opened at the Babbington Clam Council, a position as an assistant copy writer. I had restrained myself, throughout the evening, from telling Mr. Beaker that a position as an assistant copy writer at the Babbington Clam Council seemed, to me, ridiculous. Talk had turned to Burton Downey, whose new novel, *Burning Wind*, had everyone talking, including me. Finally, because the hour was so late and the meal had been so good and I had known Mr. Beaker and Eliza for so long and I had had too much to drink, I confessed.

"You know," I said, and paused to gather all their attention, "that's what I'd really like. I'd like a *Burning Wind.* I'd like to write a big, fat book, bigger than *Burning Wind.*" (Just as an aside here let me ask what it is about being young that makes us want to do things that are difficult beyond anything we know, beyond what we have even learned how to imagine, and in some cases, of which mine is one, makes us so burn to do them that we never let go of the desire to do them until at last we have done them or have failed in the attempt? Albertine's answer, when I posed this question to her, was, "We were all asses in the past," but she was busy at the time, going over the accounts, and she may not have given it much thought.)

Mr. Beaker, perhaps because he had endured with equanimity and restraint an evening of youthful ambition and egotism that must finally have had an effect like that of eating too many jelly doughnuts, and because he had endured my coolness toward the work at which he had labored for so long, work that he had hated when he had done it but had come, in the fullness of time, to regard as his apprenticeship, work that had been necessary and valuable, rose, stretched, yawned, looked down at me, and said, deliberately, "Ahhhh, but Peter Leroy will never do that."

He gave me a twisted smile, drank the last of his cognac, and got our coats while my heart sank and snow fell on my future. We said our good-nights, and we all kept our smiles on, but after that night I never spoke frankly to Mr. Beaker again.

19

NEARLY EIGHT YEARS later, I was earning my living as a writer: writing advertising copy, brochures, recipe booklets, press releases, and answers to inquiries and requests for brochures and recipe books. I was working for the Babbington Clam Council. This was, I told myself, an apprenticeship, and when asked about my work, I was quick to enumerate the many things I had learned from it. I tried not to admit to myself how much I enjoyed the work, how happy I would probably be if I were to stick at it. Instead, I spent my evenings, and stolen hours at work, trying to write that big book, and trying not to believe that Mr. Beaker might have been right, that I would never do it. But the harder I worked, the more confused and uncertain I became. I filled cartons with fragments, but of what construction they were fragments was not clear, and often when I should have been wrestling with a big idea I was wandering around Kittiwake Island.

Sitting at my desk one morning, I opened a letter from Robert Meyer, who was still wandering from place to place, accumulating degrees, writing letters, and, by his own account at any rate, breaking hearts. He had enclosed a clipping from the *International Herald Tribune,* an article about clams based on a press release that I had written. In the space of a single moment, my life's work was determined, for on the reverse of the clipping were several classified ads, in one of which a name caught my eye: Larry Peters. The publisher of the Larry Peters series was looking for people to write new installments, not only new adventures for Larry, but installments for other series as well. By responding to the advertisement, I learned that the several series of books for girls and boys published by this house were written by people working from character dossiers and plot outlines that the publisher himself supplied. When I had read the books as a boy, I had believed that they were written by Roger Drake, whose name appeared on the covers, and it never occurred to me that there were many "Roger Drakes," that the Larry Peters stories were the product of several hands, that the Roger Drake whose name appeared on each of the books was himself a work of fiction. Those stories that had appeared over the years, those stories of which I had been so fond, in which I thought I had found so much more than met the eye, beneath the text of which I thought I had been able to read a richer text about the way Larry lived with his family and his friends, the way he understood things, the way he felt about things, had been built on a deception.

Only after a careful rereading and a good deal of thought did I understand that underpinning the Larry Peters adventures, the only foundation beneath them, was what I had wanted to be there, nothing but what I had donated to Larry from my past, from my imagination. To a great degree, the Larry Peters I knew, the Larry Peters I had once wanted to be, had always been my creation, was even, perhaps, me.

I got the job advertised on the back of the clipping that Robert sent me, and for the last nine years I have been the only Roger Drake. Since the series had become dated in its topical references and in the props that the succession of earlier Roger Drakes had used, my first task was to revise all the earlier books, in sequence. Thereby, of course, I got the opportunity to bring the books more in line with what I had imagined them to be, and even to insert here and there

some of the episodes that I had imagined occur-
ring in the gaps between adventures. I have also
written eight adventures that are entirely my
own, and the income from the Larry Peters books
that I've written, added to what we make from
the hotel (which is quite small for the effort
involved) has allowed Al and me to live quite
comfortably for the last five years or so, or at
least would allow us to live quite comfortably if
we had any sense about money at all.

I am often asked whether the Larry Peters
books that I have written are autobiographical.
They are and they are not. It's not surprising, I
suppose, that the characters in my version of
Larry Peters have acquired some of the habits,
expressions, and physical characteristics of people that I have actually known. Larry's friend
Rocky King has become more and more like my
friend Raskol. Lucinda and Marie exhibit aspects
of most of the girls and women I ever had any
interest in. Larry's father and mother seem to be
composed of equal parts derived from the depic-
tions of them in the earlier Larry Peters books,
my own parents, and both sets of my grandparents. I have also included details and props from
my life in Larry's: the kittens that live beneath
the Peterses' front porch are the very kittens I
pursued on my grandparents' lawn the day that
Mr. Beaker introduced Eliza Foote to us, the day
that my mother fell out of her lawn chair. The

alabaster busts of Peterses that reside in lighted niches in the wall along the staircase are derived from the coconuts my great-grandmother carved to represent Leroys. In that capacious summer during which all the adventures occur, there is room for everything, and nothing changes much once it has been admitted into Larry's world. So, at the top of the Peterses' house, my great-grandmother lives forever, unchanging, still strong, playing the part of the matriarch of the Peters bunch, offering the guidance that so often holds the key to the solution of the mystery in each book.

The publisher has complained from time to time that the changes I have made in the series have led to the misperception of the books as being intended for adult readers, rather than for adolescents, and that the "adventures" I write for Larry are not really adventures. Well, I never thought that the Larry Peters books were intended only for adolescents, and I never thought that the adventures were very important. I try, I do try, to include in each episode something that will build suspense, but I find that as I work on, say, the stealthy approach of saboteurs who are bent on destroying the prototypes for next year's line of Peters knickknacks, my attention is easily diverted to, for example, Larry and Lucinda, who are having an interesting conversation about love and jealousy while they sit on the lowest limb of the apple tree out beyond the gazebo. Larry's adventures are more likely to be the little adventures of his growing-up, which turn out to resemble the little adventures of my own.

Yet there is, I hope, mystery of a sort. My friend Raskol, who has spent a lifetime tinkering, who has a poet's admiration for the machine that does its job with the fewest parts, the computer program that does its job with the fewest commands, who has an irresistible itch to find out how a thing works, and who can see a complex thing whole as soon as he takes the lid off it, as if he were looking at the designer's drawings, once gave me the highest praise I've received for any of my Larry Peters books. He said, and this is all he's ever said about my work, "I like the way everything snaps together at the end." Making everything snap together at the end is what makes the writing of each Larry Peters book an adventure for me; it provides the small part of writing them that is play. I've tried, most of the time, to make an object or an idea control the book, like a cotter pin, say, that appears and reappears unexpectedly—at the bottom of a drawer, in someone's pocket, hanging improbably on a gold chain—and snapping into place at the end as the pin that holds the whole gadget together. Not everyone likes that sort of thing, of course, and many of my readers have written quite persuasive letters asking for fewer cotter pins and more laughs.

20

AND THEN, some four years ago, I was sitting in Corinne's Fabulous Fruits of the Sea one night, talking to Porky White, complaining along familiar lines.

"It still isn't enough, Porky," I said. "Now that I'm Roger Drake, I ought to be satisfied, but I'm not. I still keep trying to write that big book about myself, that book as rich and various as a good clam chowder, loaded with useful and interesting information, hilarious anecdotes, recherché allusions, philosophical speculations, intriguing stories, clever word play, important themes, striking symbols, creative sex, intricate diagrams, mouth-watering recipes, big ideas—"

"Yeah," said Porky, "but you want to know something?"

"What?" I asked.

"I don't think that the guy I'm listening to now is ever going to do that."

My heart sank.

"Don't get me wrong," said Porky. "I mean

just what I said: the guy I've been listening to for
the last hour is never going to write it. He takes
himself too seriously, much too seriously to do
what you're always talking about doing. His ego
is too tender, and he protects it too well. He's too
afraid of making a mistake. He's afraid of making
a fool of himself, afraid of falling on his face in
print, afraid that people are going to laugh at
him."

There was a danger of my bursting into tears.
To hide my face from Porky, I brought my beer
mug up and drained it slowly. Porky signaled for
two more.

"Let me give you some advice," said Porky.
"You don't have to take it. What you need is a
new dummy. You've got a dummy called Larry.
Now you need a dummy called Peter. Let Peter
the Dummy write the big book." Porky held his
hand up in a gesture that meant that I should
hear him out. "Years ago, I used to listen to Bob
Balducci on the radio. You probably don't
remember him. He was a ventriloquist, and he
had a dummy named Baldy. Baldy used to say
the craziest things, insulting things, embarrassing
things, stupid things. I don't remember any of
them now, but they were crazy things; he used to
break me up. Sometimes, though, Baldy would go
a little too far: he'd say something too stupid, or
too embarrassing, or too insulting, and you know

what he'd say then? He'd say, 'The big guy made me do it.' "

Porky laughed long and loud at the memory of this remark. "And you know what Balducci would say to that? He'd say, 'Don't listen to him—he's only a dummy.' "

He laughed long and loud again, and then he pulled his handkerchief out of his pocket and blew his nose twice. He shrugged. "Maybe I'm not making myself clear," he said. But he had made himself so clear that my heart had begun to go pit-a-pat and I couldn't speak. I just sat there wearing a wacky grin.

*The Personal History, Adventures, Experiences &
Observations of Peter Leroy* is a series of novels.
Every four months a new book in the series is
released. For information about forthcoming titles,
ask your bookseller or write to:

> Apple-wood Books
> Box 2870
> Cambridge, MA 02139

Currently Available
My Mother Takes a Tumble
Do Clams Bite?
Life on the Bolotomy
The Static of the Spheres
The Fox and the Clam
The Girl with the White Fur Muff
Take the Long Way Home

Coming Soon
"The Young Tars" ... in which Peter swears an
oath.